Lamb Chops

Kelly Doudna

Illustrated by Neena Chawla

Consulting Editor, Diane Craig, M.A./Reading Specialist

ABDO
Publishing Company

Published by ABDO Publishing Company, 4940 Viking Drive, Edina, Minnesota 55435.

Printed in the United States.

Credits
Edited by: Pam Price
Curriculum Coordinator: Nancy Tuminelly
Cover and Interior Design and Production: Mighty Media
Photo Credits: AbleStock, Bigstockphoto, Corel, Digital Vision, Photodisc

Library of Congress Cataloging-in-Publication Data

Doudna, Kelly, 1963-
    Lamb chops / Kelly Doudna ; illustrated by Neena Chawla.
        p. cm. -- (Fact & fiction. Animal tales)
    Includes index.
    Summary: Bored by her daily routine, Lacy Lamb thinks outside the flock and ends up creating a wonderful surprise. Contains facts about sheep.
    ISBN 1-59679-947-1 (hardcover)
    ISBN 1-59679-948-X (paperback)
    [1. Sheep--Fiction.] I. Chawla, Neena, ill. II. Title. III. Series.

PZ7.D74425Lam 2006
[E]--dc22
                                                                                    2005024517

SandCastle Level: Fluent

SandCastle™ books are created by a professional team of educators, reading specialists, and content developers around five essential components—phonemic awareness, phonics, vocabulary, text comprehension, and fluency—to assist young readers as they develop reading skills and strategies and increase their general knowledge. All books are written, reviewed, and leveled for guided reading, early reading intervention, and Accelerated Reader® programs for use in shared, guided, and independent reading and writing activities to support a balanced approach to literacy instruction. The SandCastle™ series has four levels that correspond to early literacy development. The levels help teachers and parents select appropriate books for young readers.

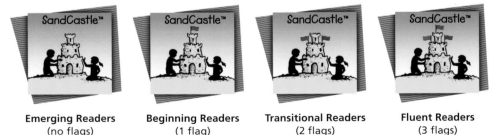

Emerging Readers	Beginning Readers	Transitional Readers	Fluent Readers
(no flags)	(1 flag)	(2 flags)	(3 flags)

These levels are meant only as a guide. All levels are subject to change.

FACT & FICTION

This series provides early fluent readers the opportunity to develop reading comprehension strategies and increase fluency. These books are appropriate for guided, shared, and independent reading.

FACT The left-hand pages incorporate realistic photographs to enhance readers' understanding of informational text.

FICTION The right-hand pages engage readers with an entertaining, narrative story that is supported by whimsical illustrations.

The Fact and Fiction pages can be read separately to improve comprehension through questioning, predicting, making inferences, and summarizing. They can also be read side-by-side, in spreads, which encourages students to explore and examine different writing styles.

FACT OR FICTION? This fun quiz helps reinforce students' understanding of what is real and not real.

SPEED READ The text-only version of each section includes word-count rulers for fluency practice and assessment.

GLOSSARY Higher-level vocabulary and concepts are defined in the glossary.

SandCastle™ would like to hear from you.

Tell us your stories about reading this book. What was your favorite page? Was there something hard that you needed help with? Share the ups and downs of learning to read. To get posted on the ABDO Publishing Company Web site, send us an e-mail at:

sandcastle@abdopublishing.com

A baby sheep is a lamb. A mother sheep is a ewe. Ewes give birth to one to three lambs at a time.

Lacy Lamb is bored. "There's nothing to do except knit sweaters," she complains.

"Knitting is what we do," says her twin brother, Leo.

5

A sheep's wool is called fleece. A sheep can grow up to ten pounds of wool in a year.

Lacy puts on a red plaid shirt. "Baa! I'm going to be a lumberjack," she says.

"That's the silliest thing I've ever heard!" Leo exclaims.

7

Sheep like to be in a group, or flock. They get nervous if they are by themselves.

"Sheep are supposed to stay with the flock. You'll be scared in the woods by yourself," Leo says.

"No I won't," Lacy declares. "When Shirley takes her afternoon nap, I'm getting out of here!"

9

Dogs are used to keep the flock of sheep together. Sometimes llamas are employed to scare wild animals away from the flock.

Shirley Sheepdog trots around the pasture. "Everything looks okay here. Nap time!" she woofs. She stretches out under a tree, yawns, and begins to count, "One sheep, two sheep …"

A sheep's stomach has four parts. Sheep eat grass and weeds. They would rather drink running water than still water.

Lacy waits until Shirley is snoring. "I'll be back by suppertime," she says to Leo. She slips under the fence and pulls her wagon up the hill.

Sheep prefer to walk uphill rather than downhill.

Every day Lacy goes up the hill to
the forest. Every day she chops down
another small tree. Every day she
wheels another log back to the pasture.

15

Sheep remember the faces of other sheep. They will still know a flock mate that they haven't seen for up to two years.

One day Lacy asks the other sheep to take a break from knitting sweaters to help her arrange the logs. "What will it be?" they wonder.

"You'll see!" Lacy says with a smile.

17

Sheep need shelter if the weather is too sunny or too wet.

Lacy and the flock stack the logs until they have built a little roadside stand at the edge of the pasture.

"Now we have a place to sell our sweaters, rain or shine!" Lacy exclaims. The other sheep smile back at her.

Leo says, "Wow, Lacy! I guess it's okay to think outside the flock after all!"

19

FACT OR FICTION?

Read each statement below. Then decide whether it's from the FACT section or the Fiction section!

  1. A sheep's wool is called fleece.

  2. Sheep chop down trees.

 3. Sheep eat grass and weeds.

 4. Sheep sell sweaters at roadside stands.

ANSWERS
1. fact 2. fiction 3. fact 4. fiction

A baby sheep is a lamb. A mother sheep is a ewe.   12

Ewes give birth to one to three lambs at a time.   23

A sheep's wool is called fleece. A sheep can grow up   34

to ten pounds of wool in a year.   42

Sheep like to be in a group, or flock. They get   53

nervous if they are by themselves.   59

Dogs are used to keep the flock of sheep together.   69

Sometimes llamas are employed to scare wild animals   77

away from the flock.   81

A sheep's stomach has four parts. Sheep eat grass   90

and weeds. They would rather drink running water   98

than still water.   101

Sheep prefer to walk uphill rather than downhill.   109

Sheep remember the faces of other sheep. They will   118

still know a flock mate that they haven't seen for up to   130

two years.   132

Sheep need shelter if the weather is too sunny or   142

too wet.   144

Lacy Lamb is bored. "There's nothing to do except knit sweaters," she complains. | 8
| 13

"Knitting is what we do," says her twin brother, Leo. | 22
| 23

Lacy puts on a red plaid shirt. "Baa! I'm going to be a lumberjack," she says. | 33
| 39

"That's the silliest thing I've ever heard!" Leo exclaims. | 47
| 48

"Sheep are supposed to stay with the flock. You'll be scared in the woods by yourself," Leo says. | 56
| 65
| 66

"No I won't," Lacy declares. "When Shirley takes her afternoon nap, I'm getting out of here!" | 73
| 81
| 82

Shirley Sheepdog trots around the pasture. "Everything looks okay here. Nap time!" she woofs. She stretches out under a tree, yawns, and begins to count, "One sheep, two sheep ..." | 88
| 95
| 104
| 111

Lacy waits until Shirley is snoring. "I'll be back by suppertime," she says to Leo. She slips under the fence and pulls her wagon up the hill.

Every day Lacy goes up the hill to the forest. Every day she chops down another small tree. Every day she wheels another log back to the pasture.

One day Lacy asks the other sheep to take a break from knitting sweaters to help her arrange the logs. "What will it be?" they wonder.

"You'll see!" Lacy says with a smile.

Lacy and the flock stack the logs until they have built a little roadside stand at the edge of the pasture.

"Now we have a place to sell our sweaters, rain or shine!" Lacy exclaims. The other sheep smile back at her.

Leo says, "Wow, Lacy! I guess it's okay to think outside the flock after all!"

120
130
138
148
157
166
176
184
192
199
209
219
220
231
239
241
251
256

GLOSSARY

fleece. the coat of wool that covers some animals

flock. a group of animals or birds that have gathered or been herded together

llama. a smaller relative of the camel that is raised for its wool and is often used to carry loads across mountains in South America

pasture. land where animals feed on grass and other plants

shelter. protection from the weather

stand. a small, open building where things are sold

wool. the soft wavy or curly hair of animals such as sheep, llamas, and alpaca

To see a complete list of SandCastle™ books and other nonfiction titles from ABDO Publishing Company, visit www.abdopublishing.com or contact us at: 4940 Viking Drive, Edina, Minnesota 55435 • 1-800-800-1312 • fax: 1-952-831-1632